P9-EMQ-651

Sue Harrington
Please return

My Grandpa Died Today

by Joan Fassler

illustrated by Stuart Kranz

Behavioral Publications, Inc.
New York

CHILDREN'S SERIES ON PSYCHOLOGICALLY RELEVANT THEMES

Titles

by Joan Fassler, Ph.D.
- ALL ALONE WITH DADDY
- THE MAN OF THE HOUSE
- ONE LITTLE GIRL
- MY GRANDPA DIED TODAY
- THE BOY WITH A PROBLEM
- DON'T WORRY, DEAR

by Terry Berger
- I HAVE FEELINGS

Manufactured in the United States of America

Library of Congress Catalog Card Number

71-147126

In memory of Grandpa Max

My grandpa was very, very old. He was much, much older than me. He was much older than my mother and father. He was much older than all my aunts and uncles. He was even a little bit older than the white haired bakery-man down the block.

My grandpa taught me how to play checkers. And he read stories to me. And he helped me build my first model. And he showed me how to reach out with my bat and hit a curve ball. And he always rooted for my team.

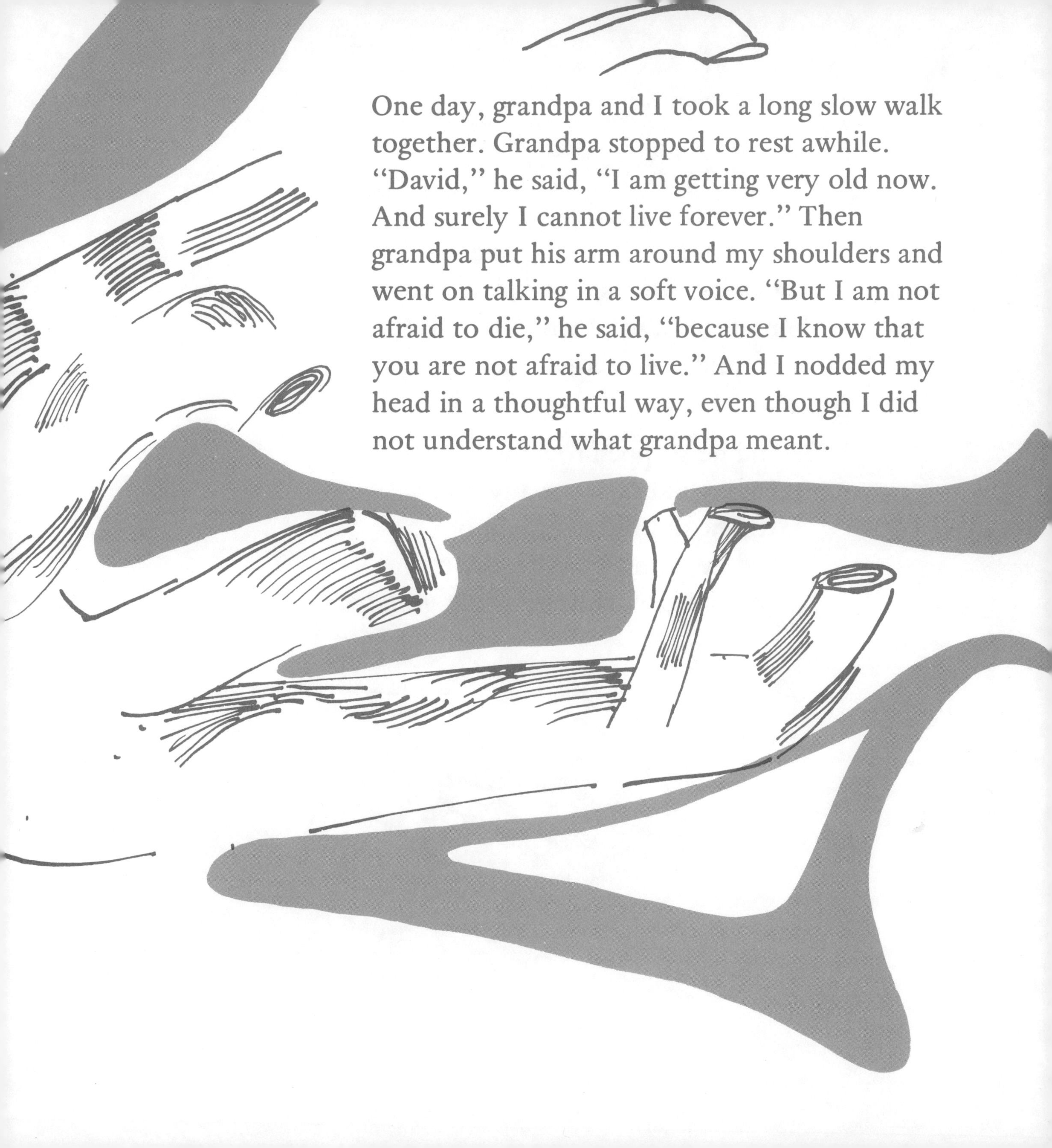

One day, grandpa and I took a long slow walk together. Grandpa stopped to rest awhile. "David," he said, "I am getting very old now. And surely I cannot live forever." Then grandpa put his arm around my shoulders and went on talking in a soft voice. "But I am not afraid to die," he said, "because I know that you are not afraid to live." And I nodded my head in a thoughtful way, even though I did not understand what grandpa meant.

Just two days later grandpa sat down in our big white rocking chair. And he rocked himself for a little while. Then, very softly, very quietly, grandpa closed his eyes.

And he stopped rocking.
And he didn't move any more.
And he didn't talk any more.
And he didn't breathe any more.
And the grownups said that grandpa died.

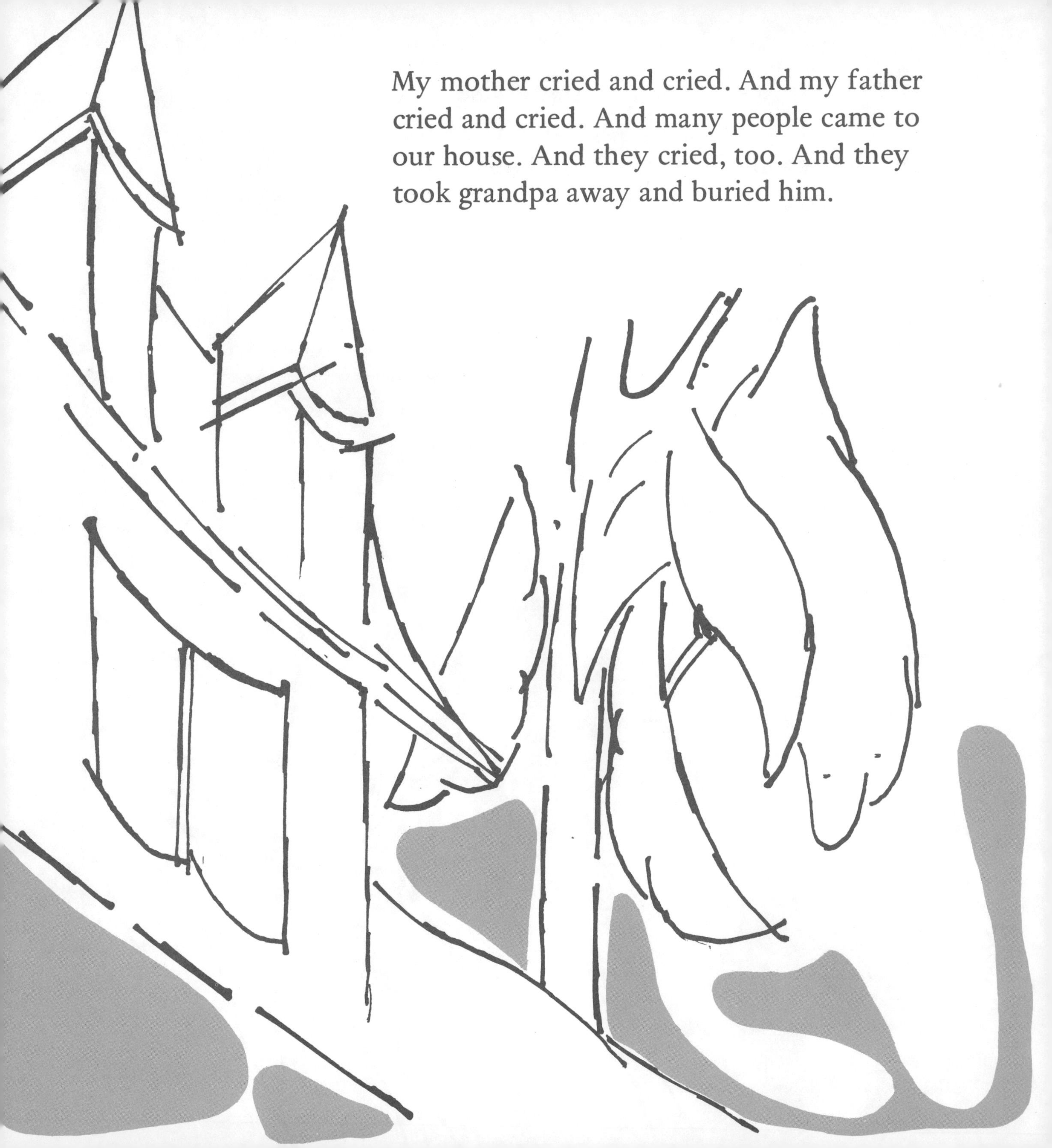

My mother cried and cried. And my father cried and cried. And many people came to our house. And they cried, too. And they took grandpa away and buried him.

More people kept coming to our house. And they pulled down all the window shades. And they covered all the mirrors. And our whole house looked as if it was going to cry. Even the red shingles on the roof. Even the white shutters at the windows. Even the flagstone steps going up to the door. And everyone was very sad.

I was sad, too. I thought about my grandpa and about all the things we used to do together. And, in a little while, I discovered a funny, empty, scary, rumbly kind of feeling at the bottom of my stomach. And some tears streaming down my cheeks.

Somehow, I didn't feel like sitting in the living room with all the gloomy grown-ups. So I walked quietly into my own room, and I took out some of my favorite toys. Then I did two jig-saw puzzles and colored three pictures. And I rolled a few marbles very slowly across the floor.

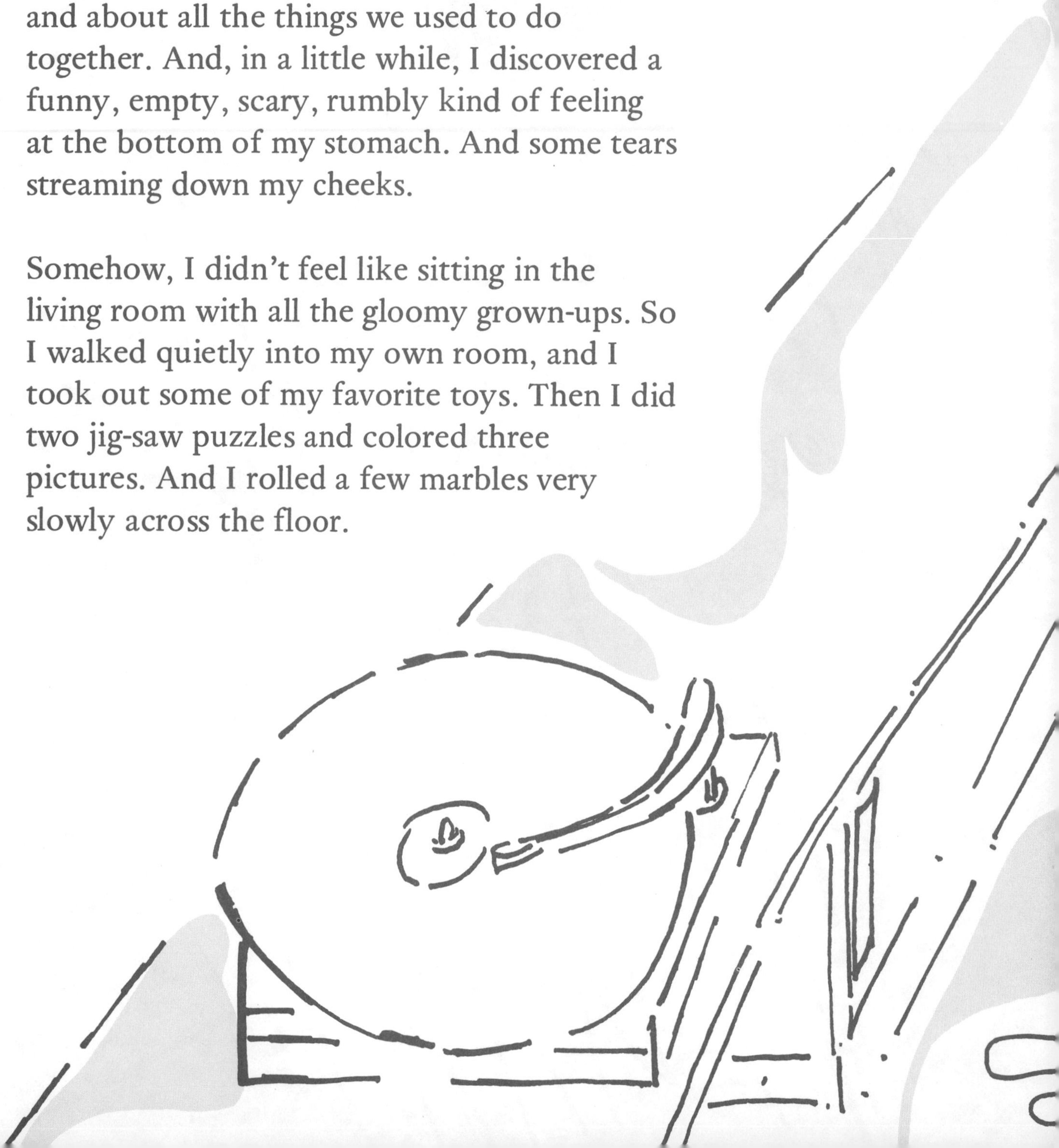

The grownups didn't mind at all. They came in and smiled at me. And someone patted me gently on my head. It was almost as if they all knew that grandpa and I must have had some very special talks together.

The next day was still a very sad day at our house. Late in the afternoon, I heard a soft knock at the door. My best friend, Bobby, wanted to know if I could play ball. And again the grownups didn't seem to mind. So I left our sad, sorry house. And Bobby and I walked slowly down to the park.

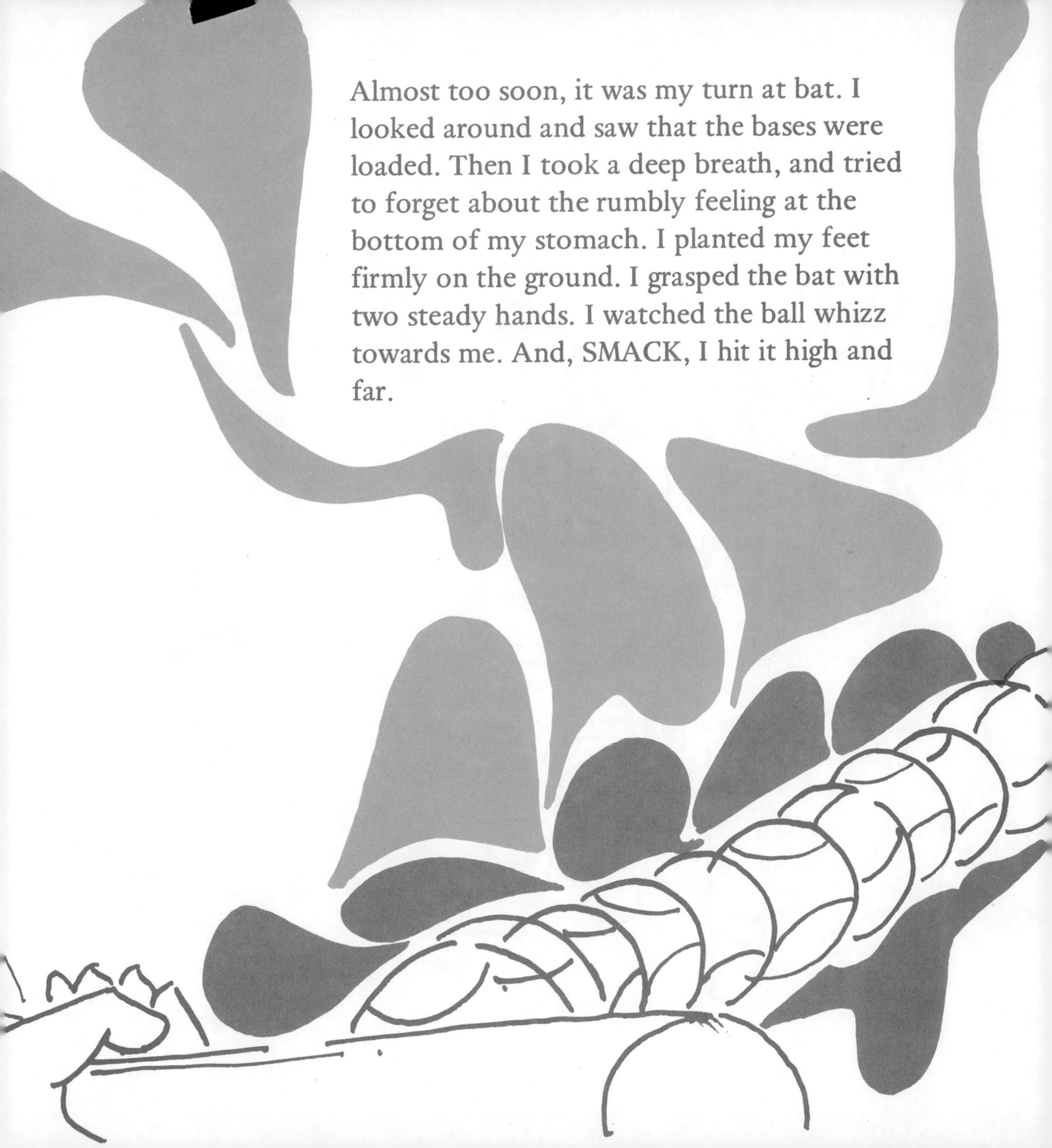

Almost too soon, it was my turn at bat. I looked around and saw that the bases were loaded. Then I took a deep breath, and tried to forget about the rumbly feeling at the bottom of my stomach. I planted my feet firmly on the ground. I grasped the bat with two steady hands. I watched the ball whizz towards me. And, SMACK, I hit it high and far.

And then I ran. I ran with every bit of strength and power and speed inside my whole body.

And it was a grand slam home run!

And somehow, right there on the field, in the middle of all the cheers and shouts of joy, I could *almost* see my grandpa's face breaking into a happy smile. And that made me feel so good inside that the rumbles in my stomach disappeared.

And the solid hardness of the ground under my feet made me feel good inside, too. And the warm touch of the sun on my cheeks made me feel good inside, too.
And, it was at that very moment, that I first began to understand why my grandpa was not afraid to die. It was because he knew that there would be many more hits and many more home runs for me. It was because he knew that I would go right on playing, and reading, and running, and laughing, and growing up.

Without really knowing why, I took off my cap. I stood very still. I looked far, far away into the clear blue sky. And I thought to myself, "Grandpa must feel good inside, too."

Then I heard the umpire calling, "Batter-up!"
And we went on with the game.